SYMBOLS of AMERICA

# The Bald Eagle

## Terry Allan Hicks

Marshall Cavendish Benchmark

Marshall Cavendish Benchmark
99 White Plains Road
Tarrytown, New York 10591-9001
www.marshallcavendish.us

All Web sites were available and accurate when this book was sent to press.

Library of Congress Cataloging-in-Publication Data
Hicks, Terry Allan.
  The bald eagle / by Terry Allan Hicks.
     p. cm. — (Symbols of America)
  Summary: "An exploration of this once endangered bird that has long served as an
  important American symbol"—Provided by publisher.
  Includes bibliographical references and index.
  ISBN-13: 978-0-7614-2133-7
  ISBN-10: 0-7614-2133-5
  1. United States—Seal—Juvenile literature. 2. Bald eagle—United
States—Juvenile literature. 3. Emblems, National—United States—Juvenile
literature. 4. Signs and symbols—United States—Juvenile literature.
  I. Title. II. Series.

  CD5610.H53 2006
  929.9—dc22
  2005020609

Photo research by Anne Burns Images

Front cover photo: Art Resource/2005 Andy Warhol Foundation for the Visual Arts/ARS, NY/Ronald Feldman Fine Arts/NY
Back cover photo: U.S. Postal Service

The photographs in this book are used by permission and through the courtesy of: *U.S. Fish and Wildlife Service:* 1, 12, 23, 27,
28, 31. *Corbis:* Peter Turnley, 4; Royalty Free, 7; Bettman, 11; Ron Sanford, 15; John Conrad, 16; W. Perry Conway, 35. *North
Wind Picture Archives:* 8. *The Granger Collection:* 19. *Peter Arnold:* Fritz Polking, 20, 24. *Visuals Unlimited:* Fritz Polking, 32.

Series design by Adam Mietlowski

Printed in Malaysia

1 3 5 6 4 2

# Contents

# CHAPTER ONE

# The American Eagle

The bald eagle is one of America's best-known symbols. This fierce *predator* stares out from the country's official seal. The eagle is also found on dollar bills and on many coins and postage stamps. The bald eagle is such an important *representative* of the nation that it is sometimes called the American eagle.

Eagles—both the bald eagle and the golden eagle—were respected and honored by many Native Americans. Some still use eagle feathers in their religious ceremonies. The early *colonists* were also drawn to these mighty birds. An eagle appears on one of the country's first coins, a copper cent minted in Massachusetts in 1776.

◀ *A Native American wearing ceremonial clothing decorated with eagle feathers.*

Charles Thomson was the first person to suggest putting the bald eagle on the Great Seal of the United States. He was the secretary of the Continental Congress and a man who knew Native American *traditions* well. He saw the bald eagle as an *inspiring* symbol of the new nation, because it was proud, powerful, and was believed to live only in North America.

*Many early Americans thought the bald eagle was the perfect symbol of their new country.* ▶

Many people did not agree with the choice. The patriot Benjamin Franklin and the famous *naturalist* John James Audubon were just two of them. They believed the eagle was a poor symbol of America. One of their reasons was that the eagle sometimes steals other animals' food, including *carrion*. Franklin wanted the wild turkey, instead. In a letter to a friend, he wrote:

[T]he bald eagle . . . is a Bird of bad *moral* character . . . like those among Men who live by sharping [cheating] and robbing . . . The turkey is a much more respectable Bird and . . . a true, original Native of America.

◄ *Benjamin Franklin was a man of many talents—a writer, a printer, a scientist, and a leader. He loved America—but not the bald eagle.*

Despite the different opinions, the Continental Congress approved the Great Seal on June 20, 1782. It shows an eagle holding an olive branch and arrows. The olive branch represents peace, while the arrows stand for strength.

Over the next 225 years, this proud creature faced a changing world. It was driven ever closer to *extinction*. The story of its return makes the bald eagle an even more inspiring symbol of the American spirit.

*The Great Seal of the United States.*  ▶

# CHAPTER TWO

# A Bird Like No Other

In the wild, a bald eagle is an amazing sight. It soars through the sky or perches high in a tree. With its yellow beak, curved *talons*, and long, white tail feathers, the bald eagle is unlike any other bird in the skies of America. It gets its name from its bright white crown of feathers. In this case, "bald" does not mean "hairless" but comes from an old word meaning "marked with white."

◄ *Bald eagles mate for life, nesting together season after season.*

Most adult males have a *wingspan* of more than 6 feet (1.8 meters). They measure about 3 feet (0.9 meters) from head to tail. The female of the species is even bigger, with a wingspan as wide as 8 feet (2.4 meters).

Despite its large size, the bald eagle is a great flier. It is able to soar on *thermals* for long periods. It can fly at speeds of 20 to 40 miles (32 to 64 kilometers) per hour. The bald eagle is also known for its powerful eyesight, four times as strong as any human's. Sharp eyes allow it to see its prey from as far as a mile (1.6 kilometers) away.

*An eagle in flight can reach heights of 10,000 feet (3,048 meters).* ▶

A skilled flier with powerful eyesight, the bald eagle is one of nature's best hunters. Fish is its favorite food. This is why the eagle is most often found near rivers, lakes, or wetlands. When an eagle sees its prey, it can dive at speeds of more than 100 miles (161 kilometers) per hour. Then, with its razor-sharp talons, it grabs the fish and flies back to its perch to eat.

◀ *A bald eagle hunts for fish in the waters off Alaska.*

Although the bald eagle prefers fish, it will eat almost anything. Ducks, turtles, rabbits, and squirrels are all part of its diet. As Ben Franklin pointed out, it will also eat animals that are already dead. Today, bald eagles are sometimes struck by cars while feeding on dead deer lying in the road.

## Did You Know?

• A bald eagle named Old Abe tagged along with the 8th Wisconsin Volunteers—which came to be known as the Eagle Regiment—in thirty-six Civil War battles.

• By law, only Native Americans who use eagle feathers for religious ceremonies may possess so much as a single one.

*Old Abe, the mascot of Wisconsin's Eagle Regiment, in a photograph taken during the Civil War.*

Bald eagles can travel over very large areas. But when the time comes to mate and hatch their young, they usually return to within 100 miles (161 kilometers) of where they were born. Bald eagles mate for life. The pairs build huge nests that they return to, and add to, year after year. These nests can be up to 10 feet (3 meters) across and weigh 2,000 pounds (900 kilograms).

*A bald eagle's nest can become so heavy that the branches holding it up break. The nest then comes crashing to the ground.*

The female lays a few eggs, usually two or three, once per year. The eggs hatch in about thirty-five days. The *eaglets* are able to fly within about three months. They can live on their own within four months. Many of the eaglets do not survive their first year, though. They are often claimed by hunger, disease, or accidents.

A bald eagle may live up to thirty years in the wild, or as long as fifty years in *captivity*. Bald eagles live in most parts of North America, from Alaska and the Canadian Arctic in the North to Texas in the South. They can also be found from Maine in the Northeast to California in the West.

The bald eagle has no natural predators. People have turned out to be its greatest threat. It was because of humans that this great flier almost became extinct.

*A two-week-old eaglet, born in captivity, waits to be placed in a nest in the wild.* ▶

# CHAPTER THREE

# Back from Extinction

In the 1700s, as many as 75,000 bald eagles lived in what was to become the United States. But over the next two hundred years, the birds faced greater and greater threats.

As America's *population* grew, people began spreading into the forests and wild spaces where eagles make their homes. The growth of America's towns and cities destroyed many of the *habitats* bald eagles have called home. Hunters, too, killed many bald eagles, either for sport or because they believed the birds harmed other animals. Large numbers of bald eagles also died of lead poisoning. The birds became sick after eating animals that had been killed by hunters using lead bullets.

◄ *The bald eagle has often struggled to survive in the modern world.*

Probably the greatest harm to bald eagles came from pollution, especially the chemical called DDT. Farmers used DDT for many years to protect their crops from insects. But the chemical made the shells of the eagles' eggs too thin and *fragile*. As a result, many eaglets could not survive.

*Scientists use instruments such as this one to measure how thick an eggshell is after an eaglet has hatched.* ▶

Slowly, through the years the bald eagle population began to shrink. Many feared that this important symbol of America was in danger of disappearing. In 1940 Congress passed the Bald Eagle Protection Act. This law made it a serious crime to kill, injure, capture, or sell a bald eagle. It was also against the law to have a single eagle feather. More than fifty years later, the *federal government* made it illegal for hunters to use shot or bullets made of lead.

◀ *An eagle returns to its nest.*

Still, by the early 1960s, the number of bald eagles living in the *lower forty-eight states* had dropped to about 450 nesting pairs. Slowly, people became more aware of the need to protect the *environment*. In 1967 the bald eagle was officially declared an *endangered species*.

The efforts to protect the bald eagle finally began to show results. The Fish and Wildlife Service helped by bringing a group of eagles to the Patuxent Wildlife Research Center in Maryland. Within a few years, the center's workers had hatched 124 bald eagles to release into the wild.

*This eagle, at Maryland's Patuxent Wildlife Research Center, is about to be released ▶ into the wild. The hood helps the bird stay calm and also protects its keeper.*

Today, the number of bald eagles continues to grow. In 1998 wildlife experts estimated that 5,748 pairs of bald eagles could be found in the lower forty-eight states. There are now nesting pairs in all but two of those states, Vermont and Rhode Island. Alaska, far to the north, is home to almost half of the world's 70,000 bald eagles. They feed on the many salmon that travel through the region.

*Three bald eagles keep watch over their feeding grounds along the Alaska coast.*

The bald eagle has had a great recovery. Someday it may be removed from the endangered species list. But this step has not been taken yet. Many wildlife experts believe the species needs even more time to build its numbers. Still, the return of the bald eagle is a success story. Its growing population shows that Americans know how important it is to keep this much-loved symbol of the nation still soaring in the skies.

*Two great symbols of America.*

▶

# Glossary

**captivity**—Life in a confined place, such as a zoo.

**carrion**—The meat of a dead animal.

**colonist**—Someone who settles in a new country.

**eaglet**—A young or baby eagle.

**endangered species**—An animal or plant that runs the risk of becoming extinct.

**environment**—The natural world.

**extinction**—When all the members of a plant or animal species have died off.

**federal government**—The government of the entire United States.

**fragile**—Weak, easily broken.

**habitat**—The place where a plant or animal makes its home.

**inspiring**—Encouraging or causing people to have strong, positive feelings or reactions.

**lower forty-eight states**—All the American states except Alaska and Hawaii.

**moral**—Knowing the difference between right and wrong.

**naturalist**—Someone who studies animals, plants, or other parts of nature.

**population**—The total number of people or animals living in a country or region.

**predator**—An animal that kills and eats other animals.

**representative**—Something that serves as a symbol or acts on behalf of a group.

**talons**—Claws.

**thermal**—A rising current of warm air.

**tradition**—A belief or way of life handed down from generation to generation.

**wingspan**—The distance between the tips of a bird's two wings.

# Find Out More

## Books

Barghusen, Joan D. *The Bald Eagle.* San Diego: Lucent, 1998.

Becker, John E. *The Bald Eagle.* San Diego: KidHaven, 2002.

DeFries, Cheryl L. *The Bald Eagle.* Springfield, NJ: Enslow, 2003.

Gibbons, Gail. *Soaring with the Wind: The Bald Eagle.* New York: HarperCollins, 1998.

Marcovitz, Hal. *The Bald Eagle.* Broomall, PA: Mason Crest, 2002.

Morrison, Gordon. *Bald Eagle.* New York: Houghton Mifflin, 1998.

Patent, Dorothy Hinshaw. *The Bald Eagle Returns.* New York: Clarion, 2000.

Quiri, Patricia Ryon. *The Bald Eagle.* Danbury, CT: Children's Press, 1998.

Wilcox, Charlotte. *Bald Eagles.* Minneapolis: Carolrhoda, 2003.

## Web Sites

The American Bald Eagle
http://www.dnr.state.wi.us/org/caer/ce/eek/critter/bird/baldeagle.htm

American Bald Eagle Information
http://www.baldeagleinfo.com

Bald Eagle
http://www.worldkids.net/eac/eagle.html

Bald Eagle Fact Sheet
http://www.kidsplanet.org/factsheets/bald_eagle.html

Bald Eagle Kids' Page
http://www.eaglestock.com/kidspage.htm

The Science Spot—Eagle Links for Kids
http://sciencespot.net/Pages/kdzeagles.html

U.S. Fish & Wildlife Service—Bald Eagle
http://endangered.fws.gov/i/B0H.html

# Index

Page numbers in **boldface** are illustrations.